Something Blue

A CLEAN INCLUSIVE ROMANCE

THE WEDDING TRIO
BOOK THREE

DAISY LANDISH

BEACHES AND TRAILS
PUBLISHING

About the Author

Daisy Landish is a romance and cozy mystery author living in the UK, whose clean and sweet stories have tugged at readers' heartstrings across the pond and beyond. When she's not writing love stories, Daisy spends her time reading, hiking at dawn, and riding into the sunset on her horse, Rosebud.

Join Daisy's Newsletter for updates and giveaways!
www.daisylandishromance.com

facebook.com/daisylandishromance

x.com/daisy_landish

instagram.com/beachesandtrailspublishing

amazon.com/author/daisylandish

bookbub.com/authors/daisy-landish

goodreads.com/Daisy_Landish

Also by Daisy Landish

Clean Regency Romance

The Lady Series - The Allington Collection

The Lady Series - The Gillingham Collection

The Lady Series - The Blackmore Collection

The Lady Series - The Norrington Collection

Clean Contemporary Romance

Love on Spruce Island

Second Chance

Cherry Tree Island

The Wedding Trio

Extra Credit

Counting on the Cowboy

Focusing on the Cowboy

Mistletoe Magic

Cozy Mysteries

Jane and Kennedy Daniels Mysteries

Pine Grove Mysteries

Annie Archer Paranormal Mysteries

Wilma Wade Holiday Mysteries

Mike and Maddie Mysteries

Mystic Moonhaven Mysteries

Sweater Weather: Cozy Mysteries for Fall

Summer Vibes: Cozy Mysteries for Summer

One

DANTE SAT and watched Sarah and Avery dancing together. The night was almost over, but the atmosphere was still electric. A tear brimmed his eyes, and his heart grew warm, sharing in their love for one another. The look on their faces when they saw the venue all decorated for the first time, the nuances and little details that spoke to them. It meant so much. It was a day they would never forget.

Dante was a hopeless romantic; he loved love. And being a part of a couple's special day meant he could experience new love all the time. Organising a wedding meant structure, organisation, lists, and everything Dante enjoyed to the fullest. All the things that helped him calm his mind and distract him from the shitty parts of the world.

Dante had been in love before. Several times actually. But he had yet to walk down the aisle himself. He was content in being a part of other people's big day, but he never fancied that day for himself. He never told anyone about how he felt. How could he explain that he loved love but never wanted to get married? What would his clients think if he told them that he believed it unnecessary and doomed to fail? It was ironic considering how much he loved planning weddings.

Dante loved hearing others' love stories and what brought them together, each such a different, exciting tale, pulling at the heartstrings and sparking hope. A hope that Dante would always ignore. Instead, he chose to live his life enjoying love without the pressures of finding *the one*. He looked at a wedding as a puzzle; he tasked himself with finding all the missing pieces to make the happy couple smile and bask in the result.

Weddings were beautiful, a time to bring people together, a time to share love and forget about everything else. It was the togetherness, the love that every person in the room shared that Dante loved; spreading happiness and joy was so important. In a world already so full of conflict and heartache, a wedding was the one time that all differences were put aside. And instead of tearing each other down, people wished the best for each other.

When he found the job at *Love and Joy*, it was a dream come true. A chance to enjoy that excitement and joy every day, a chance to immerse himself into organising and planning – his favourite things! And when Juliette had offered him ownership over part of the business after he helped it expand, he was over the moon. Something that was his that he could nurture and grow and help bring that feeling to others. It was his own. It was his calling.

Wedding and parties always made him feel special, like he was in the cool kid club. They made him feel light as air, like he might take off flying at a moment's notice. His footsteps would be lighter, and every day he would look forward to checking off a new task on his list; watching the seeds he had planted flourish into beautiful flowers. Every night he would go to bed with a sense of accomplishment and satisfaction. No other job he had worked before gave him that feeling.

Every cloud has a silver lining. But in Dante's experience, every sunny day had a cloud. It was that little voice of doubt in Dante's mind that made him wonder how long a marriage would last. He would watch the couples on their big day with hope and prayer that they would be back to plan an anniversary or celebrate the birth of a child in a few years. He hated it when he could tell a couple was getting married because they felt obligated to after being together for so long or because of family ties—those weddings were doomed to fail and reinforced the fact that Dante would never get married.

Dante helped plan every wedding that came through *Love and Joy*, and that little voice would ask him, *Have you done enough? Will this wedding be enough?* A small part of him wanted to believe that if the wedding was perfect, if the couple was so overwhelmed with joy and memories to remind them of why they chose to get married, then maybe, just maybe, that marriage would be a success.

Two

DANTE FIRST FELL in love with weddings when he was ten; when his mother and father were getting married. His parents saved their money for years to afford their wedding. And the time had finally arrived. Dante loved seeing his mother so happy, finalising all of the details, picking out a colour scheme, and smiling as she crossed off the days on the calendar.

When the day finally came, everything was beautiful. And seeing his mother and father staring at each other with nothing but love in their eyes was perfect. As Dante grew up, he would pull out their photo album and stare at the pictures, remembering all the feelings from that day.

A couple of years later, when the arguments started and his parents spent less time together, Dante relied on that little photo album more often. Memories of a happier time. His parents didn't notice it was missing, so Dante kept it hidden under his bed for safekeeping.

One night, when he woke to hear his mother crying in the kitchen, he snuck out of bed carrying the photo album in hopes of cheering her up; his heart broke when it didn't work. The following day, he woke up to find his father was gone. He never saw him again.

It was only years later that his memory of what happened that night came back. He assumed he had blocked out the memory or dreamt it. But he hadn't.

"You trapped me! I never wanted kids; I never wanted to get married. I did all that because I cared. And look what it's gotten me. I don't know who I am anymore, and that's because of *you*. Goodbye, Keira!" His father had screamed.

The years went by and Dante watched his mother try to replicate the love she had for his father. First came Darius, a doctor from Chicago. That marriage failed when he cheated. Next came Tom, the car salesman. That marriage ended because Tom worked too much, and Keira didn't like the lack of attention. The third was Jerry. He said that Keira was too needy. Each time, Keira had seemed happy and the wedding was beautiful. But the marriage never lasted. As Dante grew older and helped his mother while she cried, saying how she thought this one was the one, Dante realised that marriage wasn't something he ever wanted.

He loved weddings, love, and the beauty of romance. But the thought of feeling that love and comfort, only to sit there in heartbreak when it all fell apart was too much. Watching his mother search for 'the one,' and spending so much of her life searching for what she thought was the answer to all her problems only to be disappointed, he could not bear it. It was draining, and Dante didn't want to live his life like that.

With each marriage, Dante watched Keira change. She would lose a part of herself, and vice versa, her partner did as well. From what Dante knew of love, it was meant to be good and pure. It was a partnership, each person bringing out the best in the other. A partnership based on love and support, and being each other's strengths not weaknesses. What he saw of love from his mother's list of failed marriages was not love. When he got the job at Love and Joy, Keira had asked her son to plan her upcoming wedding. It had been the first wedding that Dante had refused to plan. He wanted no part in it.

Three

"Good morning," Dante cheered as he arrived at work.

"Someone seems extra chipper this morning," Juliette grinned.

"I'm still basking in the glory of Avery and Sarah's wedding last night," Dante sighed, settling in behind his desk with his coffee.

"It was a beautiful night. You should be proud, some of your best work yet," Juliette said, raising her mug in cheers.

"Oh please, it was a team effort. I wonder what our happy couple is up to this morning."

"Probably getting ready for their honeymoon."

Dante sighed, looking at the spot on the wall where they planned to hang the picture of Avery and Sarah's wedding day.

"I love this feeling. The day after, you know, when it's gone well. It's one of my favourite parts of this job," Dante said.

"I know exactly what you mean. We can't relax for too long. We still have plenty of other people waiting for us to make their event special," Juliette got up and stretched.

"Just a little longer," Dante chuckled, swinging back and forth in his chair.

With Avery scheduled to be off work for the next three weeks for her honeymoon, Dante and Juliette were working double time. They had planned to make more time to manage the workload, but it didn't leave much time to sit and relax. Thankfully, working through to-do lists and finding solutions to tricky situations was where Dante thrived.

When a florist had double booked for a sweet sixteenth and had to cancel, Dante found a new supplier last minute with the same floral arrangement for half the price. When save the dates arrived with the wrong names, Dante fixed it, all while making sure he and Juliette were full of coffee and well-fed.

"You are superhuman," Juliette yawned at the end of the day. "How are you still so full of energy? I'm beat."

"This is what I live for, darling, have a good night; I will see you in the morning," Dante kissed Juliette on the forehead, leaving her to lock up before heading home.

Dante woke the following morning to several texts from Juliette. There was an issue with one of the brides of a wedding they were planning. Claudia had gained a reputation from the second she walked into Love and Joy as being a bridezilla. Every detail had to be run by her and triple-checked before it was signed off on. She would call at all hours of the night and make changes once details had already been confirmed. Her wedding was fast approaching. But since everything took three times as long, Juliette was concerned that they would not have the wedding prepared on time, if the bride-to-be carried on at the rate she was going. It would be the first time Love and Joy failed to pull off an event if that happened.

"Hey, Juliette, what's up?" Dante asked as he rushed to get ready.

"It's Claudia Herman; she has had me up all night," Juliette yawned back through the phone.

"Oh dear, what is the problem this time?"

"Catering. One of her friends debunked the cater we had already chosen, something about not having enough of a following on social media. Apparently, this bride insists on only having vendors with huge followings."

"How can I help?"

"I need to get at least a few more hours sleep, and I have meetings all day, and then I have to set up the medical conference out of town. Can you contact her chosen caterer and set us a last-minute tasting?"

"Sure, email me over the details," Dante agreed, jumping in his car.

When Dante arrived at Love and joy, he sent out a few emails rearranging his appointments for the day and updated his schedule. He was determined this bridezilla would not mess up the other events he was organising. Finally, he checked the email from Juliette, and he sighed deeply in frustration. The caterer Claudia had chosen was Ben Ramos.

Dante had worked with Ben on several events before and was not looking forward to working with him again, especially on bridezilla's wedding. Ben had a reputation as being difficult to work with. And the few times Ben and Dante worked together, Ben had run late and valued his own opinion over the customers. Dante thought Ben had an inflated ego and hated the way he barked orders at everyone like they worked for him – Dante included.

"Juliette, seriously? Ben Ramos? We couldn't have found anyone else to work with on this wedding?" Dante complained as Juliette arrived.

Juliette was still sleepy and stressed; her hair was messy, and she had coffee down her blouse, yawning and brewing a fresh pot. She stretched out her shoulders and ran a frustrated hand over her face.

"I know, believe me, but she asked specifically for him. I have so much to do today, and I've spilt coffee all over myself, trying to avoid a learner driver on my way in. Can you please, *please*, deal with it for me? I don't think I have the energy for it today," Juliette yawned.

"Of course, I will. I just hope he doesn't make things harder for us."

"Me too," Juliette smiled, heading to her office to change her shirt.

Dante called Ben but only reached his voicemail. Checking his social media, Dante realised he had been out partying the night before and was most likely sleeping off a hangover. Rolling his eyes, he picked up his phone and tried the next best thing. Calling Claudia.

"Hi, Claudia. It's Dante from Love and Joy. I'm having difficulty reaching Mr. Ramos; however, I have several other caterers who offer similar menus to his. Would you like me to set up a tasting with one of those?" Dante asked as sweetly as he could summon.

"No! I specifically asked for Ben Ramos. I don't want anyone else. I'm paying you a lot of money for this wedding. How hard is it to do a simple tasting? I have so many things I need to do today. Do I need to do your job for you too?" Claudia snapped into the phone.

"Of course not; I am aware of your busy schedule and was simply hoping to offer you an alternative to work with."

"Thank you for your consideration," Claudia began, her gentle tone was a shock compared to every other interaction Dante had with her so far. "But as I said, I'm paying for a service, so get me Ben Ramos, and I need the tasting by three this afternoon. Got it?" Claudia snapped, slamming the phone down.

"Well, she's a treat," Dante muttered with a huge sigh. He took a big sip of his cappuccino, rearranged the buttons on his blazer, and mustered his inner wedding planner to continue his day.

After several more attempts, Dante finally managed to get hold of Ben's assistant and arranged the last-minute tasting, but on the grounds of a five per cent increase on his usual fee.

"Of course, he is always thinking of the money. Materialistic, childish fool," Dante mumbled.

He carried on with his day and got through as much work as he could before rushing off to the Fisher Hotel for the tasting. Dante didn't know what he was dreading more: working with Ben or bearing witness to Claudia's reaction when Ben did what Ben did best – put himself first.

Four

To Dante's surprise, Ben's team had arrived on time and was already setting up for the tasting. A printed-off menu of potential dishes lay on the tables, ready for when Miss Herman arrived. Servers were on standby, and a team of bar staff stood with bottles of wine that complimented each dish. Dante was impressed. *Perhaps Ben had turned over a new leaf. Maybe I was too quick to judge.*

But Dante was rarely wrong about anyone, and he took his job very seriously. Heading into the kitchen, he found Lucy – Ben's sous chef – but no Ben. Searching the rest of the area and the car park, he realised Ben's car wasn't there. *Typical. Late again*, Dante huffed.

As three o'clock approached, Dante began to panic. Claudia was on her way, and from the last communication Dante had with her, she was bringing two of her friends, one of whom was a known social media influencer with a vicious tongue when it came to reviews. Dante tried to call Ben again, but his call went to voicemail. Running into the kitchen, Dante looked around to see Ben's team had made a start on some of the dishes, but the main courses hadn't been touched, and they were time-consuming dishes.

"Lucy! The lamb and the salmon dishes, tell me you know how to make them." Dante pleaded, sliding out the way as chefs moved from stovetop to stovetop.

"Yeah, but Ben will not like it if I start them without him; plus, I don't have his seasoning list. He keeps them very secret. No one knows them," Lucy hurriedly answered.

"I don't care. There is no sign of him, and I can't reach him on the phone. You will just have to start without him. Miss Herman is on her way, and I will only be able to stall her for so long. We cannot afford to piss her off."

"He won't like it."

"Right now, I don't give a hoot what Ben Ramos likes. If he wanted things done his way, he should have arrived here on time," Dante snapped and turned on his heels to stall for as long as he could.

Heading back outside to try and call Ben once more, Dante watched as Claudia arrived with her friends. All three of them were dressed in almost identical all-white outfits with their Chanel purses, stiletto heels, and oversized sunglasses.

"Good afternoon, Miss Herman. You look stunning," Dante welcomed her with a light kiss on both cheeks.

"I know. I see Ben Ramos is here. I'm glad we got all that mess sorted out. Now, let's move on with this tasting; I have a lot to do," Claudia snapped her fingers, brushing past Dante and heading to the private dining room.

Dante followed close behind and helped Claudia and her friends settle in, making small talk about the wedding, hoping to stall the women long enough for Ben to arrive. But flattery and getting the women to boast and brag about themselves could only last for so long, especially with Claudia being known for having little to no patience.

"Ok, I think I have kept you gabbing for long enough. Let's get this tasting underway," Dante smiled, heading to the kitchen to check on the appetizers.

Dante panicked when he realised that Ben still had not arrived. And Lucy was no closer to having the tasters for the main courses finished. Dante was not one to panic for long. He knew little about Ben's menu but enough to ramble on about it long enough for Lucy to finish the dishes. He swooned and encouraged the ladies to enjoy their tasting, bringing them fresh summery cocktails in oversized glasses. He put on his best girlfriend bestie attitude and convinced them to picture and post the tasting on social media as it was happening.

"This *live* action capturing of your taste testing will surely attract more followers." Dante clasped his hands together and shamelessly made use of his sexy voice. Though he wished it had the same effect on male prospects, he knew straight women lapped it up.

The appetizers were a huge success, and after a lot of discussion, Claudia picked the one she wanted for her wedding. Dante tried to stall a bit longer by asking the bar staff about the wine sections.

"What about the main course?" Samantha asked, checking her watch, and becoming impatient, her mood instantly rubbing off on Claudia.

"The main courses will just be a little while longer. You know Mr. Ramos. He is a perfectionist," Dante reassured. "How about while we wait, we try out more cocktails?"

"I didn't order cocktails," Claudia said.

"No, you didn't, but as you are a special client of Love and Joy, we are offering you a complimentary cocktail hour with personalized drinks for your special day," Dante smiled.

"That sounds great. No one else will have anything like it. Cocktails that are all about *you*, it's *perfect*," enthused Natalie, Claudia's other friend.

Dante convinced the bar staff to create a list of unique, on-the-spot cocktails. And to his amazement, they pulled it off. *Motivational speaking could be my backup career,* Dante swooned to himself. They offered Claudia and her friends a quick tutorial on how to make them so they could recreate the tasty drinks even after the wedding; then they entertained them with their bottle tossing skills. Claudia and her friends ate up the show, loving every second of it, and selecting several cocktails from the made-up menu.

"I'll go check on the main courses," Dante said, hurrying off to the kitchen. With a sigh and palpable urgency in his voice as he turned the corner, he asked, "Any sign of him? How long on the dishes? *I can't stall much longer.*"

"You will have to," was Lucy's only reply.

Taking a deep breath and putting on the biggest smile, Dante headed back to Claudia and her friends. Preparing to make his excuses and stall, Dante was surprised when the kitchen doors swung open and Ben hurried in, pushing a tray with four main course options. The aroma of thyme, rosemary, salmon, and Ramos' signature red wine sauce filled the room, making Dante's stomach rumble and his mouth water.

"Dinner is served," Ben pronounced in his handsome voice.

Dante tried to hide his annoyance. But Ben caught the look and offered him a cheeky smile and a wink in response.

"Miss Herman. I present baked salmon with zucchini and herb salad, and slow-roasted lamb shoulder with my signature secret red wine marinade. Looking at your choices for wine, cocktails, and appetizers, I have also made two more options I think you will love to try. I have ginger and secret herb prawns with roasted rice. Lastly, I have prepared buffalo ricotta and basil zucchini flowers with asparagus and a prosecco dip." Ben smiled, laying the dishes out for the women to try.

"Oh my *god*, these are amazing. I know I had made the right choice picking you," Claudia cheered while all social graces went out the window as she gobbled the wonderful food.

The ladies tucked into Ben's delicious foods, and Dante and Ben excused themselves to prepare for the dessert tasting. Once they were alone in the kitchen, Dante could no longer bite his tongue.

"What time do you call this? Are you *completely* incompetent? You got lucky this time, but if you pull a stunt like this again, I can assure you Love and Joy will *never* work with you again." Dante snapped.

"Relax, Guapo. I got here on time. I was preparing the main course. I knew my team could handle everything else," Ben said plainly while plating a rhubarb and gingerbread truffle.

"You got lucky. If Miss Herman keeps you on for her wedding, I expect you to be *on time* from here on out," Dante insisted.

"Por favor Guapo, don't worry so much; it will give you wrinkles. And you are far too good looking for that," Ben winked, blowing a kiss in Dante's direction.

"Oh please, just do the job we are paying you for, and don't mess this up," Dante rolled his eyes and headed out to Miss Herman and her friends.

Delighted with the selection of foods and how Dante went above and beyond to please her and her friends, Miss Herman left, having picked her final food, drink, and cocktail list for the wedding. She kissed Dante on both cheeks while getting ready to leave.

"Thank you, Dante. Believe me, all our followers will hear about the wonderful job Love and Joy did here today. I am so excited about the big day, talk soon. Adios," Claudia waved.

Finally allowing himself to breathe, Dante headed back inside. Dante emailed the finalised food selection to Ben and Juliette and called Juliette to send the completed contracts over to Ben. Running his hands over his face, Dante sat, taking the weight of his feet that had suddenly begun to ache.

"Here, try this. You look like you need it," Ben offered, handing Dante a cocktail.

"I'm driving," Dante answered.

"It's virgin," Ben replied.

Dante took the drink and choked back at how strong it was.

"That was *not* a virgin cocktail," Dante spluttered.

"I thought you could do with relaxing. You look so tense, Guapo. Take a load off and have a drink with me."

"I don't think so. I will have the contracts for the Herman wedding emailed to your office right away. Do not delay in signing them." Date packed his bag and shrugged on his jacket.

"Whatever you say, Guapo."

"And *stop* calling me Guapo," Dante yelled as he left the room.

Five

EVERYTHING WAS in order for Claudia's wedding. The event was only a few weeks away and the guests had all rsvp'd. The wedding cake design had been finalised, the dresses and suits had been altered, and the venue had accepted the changes and the expanded guest list. Juliette and Dante had received no more late-night calls from Claudia, and all was well.

Avery had arrived back from her honeymoon and took control of the planning, giving Juliette and Dante a few well-deserved days off. Dante travelled out of town to spend some time with his mother, who insisted on his opinions about her wedding, but Dante was adamant he wouldn't help. He had enough issues surrounding marriage because of his mother's past, and he didn't want her to spoil his love of wedding planning. When Avery called, Dante was happy to end his trip early.

"Sorry to ask, but Miss Herman is insisting you help with this as you did so well last time," Avery said.

"It's okay, to be honest, I'm happy for the distraction. What's the problem this time?"

"You are not going to like this, but she wants to arrange another tasting with Ramos," Avery cringed.

"You have *got* to be kidding; we finalised the menu weeks ago," Dante complained.

"I know, apparently another one of her friends needs to give her stamp of approval."

"What is it with this woman and her constant need for her friend's approval? It is her wedding, isn't it?" Dante thought of Ben and how handsome he looked gliding around the kitchen preparing the desserts.

"I know. Do you want me to make the arrangements with Ramos?"

"*Please*. Dealing with him on the day is going to be bad enough," Dante sighed.

"I'll text you the details," Avery laughed, ending the call.

The following day, Dante arrived at the hotel to find Claudia and her friend Michelle already waiting. Taking them inside, Dante knew it would be a difficult day. Michelle appeared to be making all the decisions, and Claudia sat back, saying nothing. Dante worried that everyone else was taking over her wedding. He wanted to talk to Claudia alone, but Michelle was like an annoying gnat who wouldn't leave her side. Things went from bad to worse when Ben and his team still hadn't arrived fifteen minutes after the scheduled arrival time.

"Where is he? Can't you control your staff?" Michelle complained.

"I'm sure it's just traffic; I will call again. I am so sorry for the delay," Dante said, rushing to call Ben, who refused to answer.

Dante kept a close eye on Claudia and Michelle while getting Ben on the phone. They looked deep in conversation, and Michelle grew more and more animated. Dante could sense there was about to be an argument. Finally getting in touch with Lucy, Dante was relieved to find that Ben was on his way and had all the food ready and prepared with him.

"I'm so sorry for the wait, there was a little van trouble delaying Mr. Ramos, but he is on his way. Is there anything else you would like to discuss about the wedding before he arrives?" Dante asked.

"Yes, actually. I don't think you are right for my wedding after all. How hard is it to get a caterer here on time for a tasting? This is not the first time he has been late. Don't think I am stupid. I know you were stalling us last time. If he isn't here in the next ten minutes, I am pulling my wedding from Love and Joy, and I will make sure you never get a booking in Summershore again. I have almost a million social media followers, and my friends have even more. We will destroy you," Claudia snapped.

Looking over at Michelle, Dante could see her smile; she approved of the overreaction. It was apparent these words were hers and not Claudia's.

"With all due respect, Miss Herman, this is a risk you run when choosing one of the most popular and influential caterers. Mr. Ramos is a very busy man. Before we started working with him, did I or did I not suggest another caterer? You insisted on working with him. I will admit his timekeeping does need some work, but as you can see from his social media, he has never disappointed any of his clients," Dante assured, trying his best to control his temper, which boiled with every second.

"Excuse me? She is your client; how dare you talk to her like that!" Michelle snapped.

"He was respectful, Michelle, calm down......she has a point, though. I am your client, it is your job to please me, and I am not pleased right now. Give me one good reason why I shouldn't pull my wedding?" Claudia demanded.

"Because if you pull from Love and Joy at this time, you will not be able to get your wedding organised in time by anyone else. Also, you are in the best hands. Otherwise, you wouldn't have trusted them with your event. And finally, if you fire Love and Joy, I will refuse to cater your wedding, and I can assure you my social media following is much bigger than yours and your friends combined," Ben said evenly.

None of them had noticed when Ben had arrived. A smile started warming Dante's lips as he appreciated Ben stepping in to help. Michelle and Claudia sat back, keeping silent. Dante worried that while Ben meant well, he may have taken it a step too far.

"How about we start again? We at Love and Joy appreciate your business, and we want to make your wedding as beautiful as possible. So, how about we get this tasting underway because I don't know about you, but I am *starving*," Dante joked.

"You're joining the tasting?" Michelle asked with disapproval, "I'm sorry, but are you coming to the wedding?"

"Michelle, shut up, and let's just get this over with. Mr. Ramos, do you have the new vegan menu prepared?" Claudia snapped.

"Ready and waiting, I shall bring it right through," Ben said, bowing his head.

After discussing the menu with Claudia, Ben and Dante found that she was only changing to a vegan menu because of her overbearing friends, and she preferred the original. Ben could see how stressed she was, and Dante worried that she was losing her love of the wedding. Trying to help Claudia with Michelle in the room was proving difficult. She disapproved of everything that wouldn't be her choice and spent most of her time on her phone.

"How about we prepare the three-course meal of your choice for the main wedding party and the other guests receive tasters of the entire selection. That way, your vegan friends are happy, your nonvegan friends do not feel left out, and everyone can try both options if they choose? I can also prepare a buffet for later in the evening," Ben offered.

"That sounds expensive. Are you sure you can afford that?" Michelle tsked.

"I can do it for the same price, and as an apology for my tardiness, I will also include a free dessert bar and silver service performing wait staff. How does that sound?"

"Perfect, thank you, Mr. Ramos, and thank you, Dante," Claudia smiled.

Michelle headed outside, animatedly talking on her phone to a new sponsor for her social media channel, leaving Ben, Dante, and Claudia alone.

"Thank you for being so patient with me. I know I haven't been the easiest bride to deal with. I'm just starting my social media career, and my friends have made it such a success. I've been on relying on them for help. What started as a little advice has run away with itself," Claudia admitted.

It was the first time since meeting Claudia that Dante thought he saw the real her.

"It's fine, dear. That's what I am here for, to help remove some of that stress. So, you just leave all the details to me. I understand you want your friend's help, but remember, this is *your* wedding, not the rest of the world's," Dante smiled. He so loved to help brides enjoy their wedding day. This is where Dante really shined. It was tough for Ben not to notice the sparkle in his eyes.

Six

DANTE PULLED out his laptop and made the amendments to the contracts for Ben and Love and Joy, while Ben cleaned up in the kitchen. After talking with Claudia a little more, Dante relaxed with confidence that the rest of the event would run smoothly.

Ben came back in with plates of food and drinks on a large trolly. Sitting opposite Dante, he watched him with a slight smile, waiting for Dante to finish. Closing his laptop, Dante sighed and relaxed back in his seat, content that his day was over, and he didn't have to worry about anything else until tomorrow.

"Thank you for your help today. I appreciate it. Miss Herman is a huge client for Love and Joy, and with her threats to ruin the business when we have only recently expanded? To say I was stressed is an understatement," Dante grinned.

"It's okay. We small business owners need to stick together. Plus, she was out of line, and you handled yourself pretty well."

"No, that was all *you*. How much will you lose making that extra buffet?"

"Ah, don't worry about it. Not enough to make me lose sleep. Here. Eat," Ben said, serving up some food.

"I'm fine, thank you."

"No. You have been here all day. Eat, relax," Ben smiled, pouring them both a glass of red wine.

The food was delicious, and Dante was thankful for the treat. He never got a chance to enjoy the food samples and had never tried Ben's food before. Each mouthful was packed with flavour, and Dante realised just how talented Ben was. He finally saw why he was so popular, and why Miss Herman made such a fuss about wanting him for her wedding.

"You are very talented. This is ridiculously good," Dante said, cleaning his mouth with one of the cotton napkins.

"Gracias Guapo," Ben grinned. "I have had a passion for cooking since my Abuela taught me how to cook when I was very young. A lot of my recipes I learned from her. It's why my secret marinades and spice lists are kept so secret. I get to share a part of her with everyone I cook for, but her recipes are just something I get to enjoy. Special memories for me, like she is still here."

"That's beautiful," Dante said.

He could see Ben's passion and love for his craft. The more they talked, the more Dante realised why Ben was always late. He preferred to do his cooking in his own kitchen so he could remember his grandmother. It was so sweet, and it softened Dante's opinion of Ben quite a lot. But there was still a lot about him that Dante couldn't get past, like how Ben talked to his staff and anyone else who chose to work with him. Though his team never seemed to mind. They knew it was just Ben trying to keep the event running smoothly. However, Dante still didn't like it.

"Allow me to help clean up," Dante said, helping clear the table.

"Oh no, it's fine, really," Ben smiled, taking the plates and stacking them on the trolly.

"I insist. It's the least I can do for your help today."

Ben fell quiet, a smile crept across his face. He folded his arms across his chest, and he cocked his head to one side. Dante felt himself blush under Ben's gaze but couldn't stop himself from grinning in return.

"What?"

"If you really want to thank me, you can do something better than washing the dishes. Would you go on a date with me? Por favor?" Ben asked.

Seven

DANTE HAD TOLD Ben he would think about it but kept dodging his calls. He had fun the night of the tasting, more than he would have ever thought. But there were many things he couldn't get past. It wasn't just the way Ben talked to his staff, or the constant lateness and not answering calls; it was his partying. Ben was ten years younger than Dante, and Dante felt too old to be going out partying at every opportunity.

Ben had his good moments. That was undeniable. He frequently sent freshly prepared lunches to Love and Joy, and coffee, and dropped off specialty cakes there himself on occasion. Juliette and Avery slowly became quite fond of Ben and looked forward to his little gift parcels.

"Oh, my days, Dante, your new boyfriend is going to make me fat. This food is too delicious. I can't stop eating," Avery joked, taking another bite of her Tarta de Santiago.

"How many times do I have to tell you? He is *not* my boyfriend. He is just very persistent in wanting a date."

"Have you given him an answer yet?" Juliette asked between bites of bruschetta.

"No," Dante replied.

"Because you like him and are loving the attention? I can't say I blame you. I love all these little treats too," Juliette grinned.

"No......" Dante began but couldn't finish.

Why hadn't he said no officially? Did he like Ben? Truthfully, Dante didn't know how he felt. But now that Juliette had pointed it out, he realised every time Ben turned up and flashed his piercing eyes and perfect smile, Dante's stomach twisted. But that was simply the flattery, right?

"Honestly, I don't know how I feel about him. He is arrogant, constantly late, expects everyone to work on *his* schedule, talks to his team with such anger and frustration, and is a little cocky...."

"But?" Avery said with a mouthful of Victoria sponge cake.

"But the day of the tasting, I saw a new side to him. He jumped to my defence when Claudia went bat crap crazy, and he told me the sweetest story about his grandmother. He is a perfectionist and loves what he does; his passion is intoxicating."

"Sounds familiar," Juliette laughed, pointing in Dante's direction.

"*Excuse me?*" Dante exclaimed in mock surprise.

"You are a perfectionist, and your passion is evident for anyone to see. You sat here for half an hour the morning after Avery's wedding basking in the after-event high." Juliette laughed.

Dante stuck his tongue out teasingly and wrinkled his nose. Juliette had a point; perhaps he wasn't that much different from Ben after all. But was that enough reason to go on a date with him? Was Dante even ready to date again so soon after breaking up with David? Something just didn't feel right, be it Ben or the timing.

"What's the worst that can happen? You go on a date; you're not feeling it; you call it quits. But.... if you like it, you arrange date number two. Who knows, I might be organising your wedding sooner than you think," Avery encouraged.

"I don't know. I'm not feeling that spark, you know? The feeling when the prospect of a first date arises, that rush of endorphins, the butterflies. Surely, that's a sign it's not meant to be," Dante tried to dismiss the thought.

"How will you know if you don't try?" Juliette asked.

"You can't keep leading the guy on Dante. Either call him and arrange a date or call it off. It's unfair to give him false hope, and all this food must be costing him a fortune," Avery said softly.

"Fine, I'll call him," Dante sighed, realising that Avery was right.

Eight

"HOLA GUAPO, it's nice to hear your voice finally. I thought you were avoiding me for a while there," Ben smiled into the phone.

"Hi Ben, if I'm honest, I was avoiding you. I didn't know how I felt about going on a date," Dante began, choosing his words wisely.

"I admire the honesty; it's a hard trait to find in people these days."

"Yes, well, I always say honesty is the best policy. So, about that date?"

"Sure, I'll make the arrangements. When are you free?"

"Most nights after six-thirty."

"Excellent. I'll text you the details."

Ben texted back the following afternoon with the details. He didn't say specifically what he had planned. The message said to meet him at The Golden Coffee Bean at seven Thursday night. Dante tried to dig for more information. He didn't want to dress too casually if Ben had something fancy planned, but he also didn't want to get too dressed up if they were simply going for coffee. Ben found Dante's worrying amusing and kept replying simply with "wear what makes you feel comfortable."

As the date approached, Ben's little gifts of food didn't stop, and Dante slowly began to open up and stop avoiding his messages. The more he talked with Ben, the more he looked forward to spending some time getting to know him. It took a lot for Dante to let his guard down, but somehow Ben was taking the wall down brick by brick with great ease and little effort. And lots of chocolate, where Avery and Juliette were concerned.

Thursday arrived, and Dante brought his date outfit to work with him for Juliette and Avery's stamp of approval. After the shop closed, Dante quickly changed and came out to wolf whistles from the girls.

"You look hot, Papi," Avery smiled, fanning her face.

Since the girls had noticed how Ben constantly called Dante Guapo, they had taken to calling him, Papi. At first, Dante hated it. But soon it grew on him, and he stopped complaining. His outfit was simple yet smart, dark jeans, a crisp white shirt, and a navy-blue blazer. He had been meaning to book an appointment with the eye doctor for weeks, and as his eyes were hurting, he ditched his usual contacts for a pair of light grey framed glasses.

"I hate wearing these things; they make me look so old," Dante complained.

"Not old. Distinguished and handsome!" Juliette smiled.

"Guapo, as Ben says," Avery winked.

For some reason, Dante was more nervous than he expected. Since he had half an hour before he was due to meet Ben, Juliette and Avery stayed behind to have a glass of wine with him to help settle his nerves.

"You will be fine, it's not like it's a blind date, and he is obviously interested in you. If someone had dodged me the way you dodged him, I would have ghosted a long time ago," Juliette said.

"Ghosted?" Avery and Dante asked in unison.

"It's what the kids say, it means.... well, vanished? Acted like a ghost and left," Juliette shrugged.

"Someone is trying to be cool for the kids. Does this have anything to do with Milo's new girlfriend?" Avery asked.

"What, girlfriend?!" Juliette said, suddenly sitting bolt upright in her chair, almost spilling her wine.

Avery and Dante burst out laughing.

"While I would love to stay and chat more about this, I have a date. Ladies, I wish you both a good evening," Dante hugged them both tightly, offering his signature kiss on each cheek and one on the forehead.

"Have fun; we want all the gossip tomorrow," Avery waved.

Ben stood waiting outside, leaning against the wall. The age difference had never been more apparent. Ben wore loose baggy jeans, a dark polo shirt, and a hooded jacket under a thick leather jacket. Suddenly, Dante felt self-conscious.

"Guapo, so good to see you," Ben cheered when he spotted Dante approach, opening his arms up for a hug, which Dante accepted nervously.

"Good to see you too; you look great. So, what's the plan for the evening?" Dante asked.

Ben pushed open the door, holding it open for Dante. Smiling softly, Dante headed inside. *The Golden Coffee Bean* was like he had never seen it before. A circle of sofas had been created in the centre of the room with all the tables and chairs rearranged around it. The lighting had changed to a soft, warm glow, candles centred on each table, and people hurried to their seats.

Taking a seat, one of the baristas, now dressed in a smart shirt and tie, came to take drink orders. Dante had never realised that *The Golden Coffee Bean* served alcohol after six p.m.

"What is all this?" Dante asked.

"What? You work just up the street and don't know about the *Coffee Bean After Dark*?" Ben asked, "Every night, after closing, *The Golden Coffee Bean* hosts a list of events, including open mike night, poetry readings, book launches, etc. I'm really surprised you didn't know since you work in event planning."

"I guess they organise their own events, and I'm so busy planning others I only come here in the morning. I can't believe I never knew this," Dante said in amazement, looking at how even the pictures on the walls had been changed.

Jazz singers playing saxophones, artists at their isles, poets reading their work. Each picture displayed all the people who had performed there in one way or another. Dante noted that he must bring Juliette and Avery there one night soon; it was precisely the type of thing they would enjoy.

"So, what's on the roster for tonight?" Dante asked gratefully, accepting his Chardonnay from the server.

"Poetry readings followed by Saxophone Steve's soft Jazz," Ben answered.

Dante watched in awe as each poet stood up and bore their soul to a room full of strangers. Each person's words touched Dante differently, bringing a tear to his eye. It was a beauty he had never experienced before. He was in a familiar setting under completely new circumstances. He struggled to control himself as each person finished their reading. Everyone clapped gently, but inside, Dante was on his feet, yelling bravo.

"Next tonight, we have a debut poet. Please give a Golden welcome to Mr. Ben Ramos," said the host.

Dante's head spun round in surprise as he watched Ben stride up to the mic in the centre of the room with such confidence and ease.

"Thank you, everyone. The piece I will be reading tonight is called *Abuela tú me hicitie* – Grandmother, you made me," Ben said, standing upright and closing his eyes.

Dante's heart pounded in his chest; he sat in anticipation, waiting, listening to Ben take a few steady breaths behind the microphone.

"*No seria quien soy sin ti.* I wouldn't be who I am without you. You made me who I am, Abuela...."

As Ben drifted into his own world. Speaking his truth, Dante felt the words. As Ben drifted from Spanish to English, Dante didn't need a translator. The emotions translated his words for him. Dante felt a moment of guilt; he had misjudged Ben far too harshly.

"*De Tu Amado Nieto.* From your loving Grandson. *Te Extrano*

Abuela......Thank you," Ben bowed his head and smiled as the room erupted in applause.

"Ben, that was.... *Hermoso*. I will admit you surprised me. I never expected this to be our first date." Dante smiled.

"A good surprise?"

"The best.... when did she pass?" Dante asked gently.

Ben looked over at him, stunned for a moment.

"*Te extrano?* It means I miss you. I'm not fluent, but I know enough."

Ben smiled back, rubbing a nervous hand across the back of his neck. Taking a big gulp of his beer, he sat staring at the bottle for a few moments, the pair ignoring the young girl now taking the mic.

"Five months ago," Ben finally admitted.

"I'm so sorry," Dante reached out and squeezed Ben's hand.

Ben continued to tell Dante how his parents had passed in a car accident when he was young, and his grandmother raised him. She wanted him to be strong and independent, so she taught him how to cook. He juggled maintaining his business and caring for her when she got sick. That's when the last puzzle piece fell into place. All of Ben's lateness and insistence on cooking in his kitchen and not on site, *everything*. It's because he was grieving. Dante felt sick that he had judged Ben before hearing his story. He offered a heartfelt apology, but Ben insisted it was fine.

"I would have done the same. Truth be told, when I first met you, I thought you were a little snobby.... but then, the more I watched you, I saw you were just like me, a perfectionist who wants to make people happy. You do it by planning their events; I do it with food." Ben smiled.

"I guess we are a lot alike," Dante mused.

"I feel like we are being rude," Ben whispered with a wink.

Dante blushed and turned back to watching the poets. Truth be told, he was enjoying listening to them all. Slowly, Ben reached across and took Dante's hand in his. Dante felt his skin prickle at Ben's touch. It was a feeling he hadn't had in the longest time. He liked how his fingers felt in between Ben's and continued to sit smiling, just content to be in his company.

"I had a really lovely time tonight," Dante smiled as they stood outside.

"I did too, so is it too forward of me to ask for a second date? Perhaps dinner?" Ben asked.

"I'd like that," Dante said with a grin.

As Dante waved goodbye to Ben and headed home, he couldn't help but think how Avery and Juliette had both been right. He was so happy he had listened and given Ben a chance.

"Oh my, that's so romantic," Avery gushed as Dante retold the night's events.

"So when is the second date?" Juliette asked.

"Friday, he is cooking me dinner," Dante answered.

Ben and Dante texted, called, and Ben popped into the store a few times throughout the week. Each time, Dante felt his feelings for Ben grow stronger. Every time the doorbell rang, he would pop his head over his computer monitor like a meerkat, hoping to see Ben walk through the door. When he saw Ben's name pop up on his screen, he would feel flushed, and goosebumps would prickle every inch of his skin.

It wasn't until Friday morning that Dante realised he had felt those feelings before. Many years ago, with the only guy Dante had ever gotten close enough to almost marry. Daniel had vowed never to speak to Dante again after calling off their wedding, saying Dante had broken his heart and led him on.

As feelings of guilt that Dante thought he had buried long ago came flooding back to the surface and the clock ticked down to six-thirty, Dante panicked. And instead of heading to Ben's place for their date, he turned off his phone and ran out of town.

Nine

BEN STOPPED SENDING his gifts and stopped contacting Dante. After how successful the first date went, Juliette and Avery were surprised. But unfortunately, Dante neglected to tell them what happened; that he felt he had messed things up by standing Ben up.

As the days passed by, Dante's guilt grew; it was obvious he had upset Ben. And that was the last thing he wanted to do. Dante had become scared of how quickly his feelings for Ben grew and simply freaked out. He kicked himself for it. He was old enough to know better and should have communicated his concerns or called for a rain check. Instead, he chose to run and hide.

"Dante, how much do you love me?" Avery asked, putting on her sweetest face and batting her eyelashes.

Dante pulled his glasses down his nose and looked over at Avery. It had become her thing to ask everyone how much they loved her while mimicking her daughter's best puppy dog look when she needed something. Juliette and Dante feigned irritation when in actual fact, they found it adorable.

"What do you want now?" Dante joked as Avery twiddled her hair between her fingers.

"Bridezilla is on the phone; she wants another tasting of the selected menu with another friend of hers."

"You can't be calling her bridezilla," Juliette protested.

"Well, I don't, to her face," Avery laughed.

Dante stuck out his hand and waited for Avery to hand him the phone. Then, mouthing 'thank you' before bowing and shimmying back over to her desk, Avery handed Dante the phone.

Dante answered, taking a breath, putting on his biggest smile, and taking Claudia off hold.

"Good afternoon, Claudia. How may I help you?" Dante asked.

"My friend Louisa wants to sample the menu. Can you arrange another tasting?"

"Miss Herman, you are aware it is far too late to be making any changes with the wedding being just days away?"

"Excuse me? I get what I want, and you do as you are told. Now arrange the tasting and do what I pay you for. Louisa is a very influential socialite with a huge following; you do not want to piss her off."

"We don't, or you don't?" Dante muttered.

"Sorry, I can't hear you. Are you arranging the tasting?" Claudia snapped.

"Post width, ma'am," Dante ended the call and fired off an email to Ben's assistant.

"Looking forward to seeing Ben again?" Juliette asked.

Dane sighed deeply, "Not really. I kind of stood him up on our second date."

"*What*?" Juliette and Avery squealed in unison.

"How do you 'kind of' stand someone up?" Juliette asked.

"I freaked out and headed to my mother's for the night," Dante answered, cringing behind his computer, waiting for their reaction.

"That's not kind standing him up. Dante, you full-on blew him off," Avery chimed.

"I know, it's bad. The thing is, I actually really like him. It's just.... I don't know... it's complicated."

"Well, it's about to get a whole lot more complicated," Juliette tutted.

To Dante's surprise, Ben and his team had arrived early, and the tasting was ready and waiting for Claudia's arrival. Dante had hoped Ben would be late as usual so he could brace himself and prepare. *Straight into the lion's den, it is then,* he thought.

Dante offered Ben a smile and a wave when he entered the dining hall, but all he received in return was a quick head nod of acknowledgement. The nonchalant gesture made Dante realise he had really messed up. The tasting continued, thankfully, without a hitch and Ben acted as if nothing had happened. Dante began to worry he had indeed hurt Ben's feelings. Ben wasn't acting cold, but he also wasn't his usual flirtatious self, and Dante missed the subtle flirtations of Ben calling him Guapo.

"Thank you for being so accommodating. I haven't been the easiest bride to deal with, and you have gone above and beyond to accommodate my demands. I will make sure to rave about Love and Joy to all my friends and my ever-growing following," Claudia smiled, giving Dante a tight hug.

Her sudden change in character had Dante's head spinning; he never knew what to expect from her. Yet he appreciated her random acts of kindness. Seeing the pressure she was under to be perfect and to live up to her friends' expectations made Dante feel sorry for her. He remembered seeing his mother going through a similar thing with her in-laws on her third wedding. Watching his mother and Claudia experience the joy being sucked out of their wedding made him more determined to get all the details right. He felt for Claudia. If she was experiencing this pressure now, he worried about the state of her marriage; he didn't want history to repeat itself like it had with his mom. Despite her snippiness and occasional unkind remarks, Claudia was a lovely girl under it all.

"Happy to help, dear. I am always here to help you make your day the best it can be. And just remember, it is *your day,*" Dante winked.

Claudia offered him a kiss on each cheek before heading over to thank Ben. Dante busied himself on his laptop while subtly watching Ben and Claudia talk. Ben was smiling, laughing, and being the Ben that

Dante had seen on their first date. He knew what he had to do. He had to apologize and ask for a second chance.

After Claudia left, Ben didn't give Dante a second look before heading into the kitchen. It hurt Dante, but he knew he deserved the cold shoulder. Taking a few moments to pluck up the courage and work on his speech, Dante hurried to finish his notes from the tasting. He emailed everything over to Avery and sent the new menu layout to Claudia to approve. *It's now, or never,* Dante thought, clenching and unclenching his trembling hands.

Opening the door to the kitchen, he peeked inside to see Ben cleaning the countertops alone. Dante didn't know when, but the rest of Ben's team had headed home for the evening. The radio was playing low from the top shelf above the sink, a Spanish radio station that Dante hadn't heard before. The door closing behind him alerted Ben to his presence, but Ben didn't look up to acknowledge Dante's arrival; instead, he headed to the sink and turned up the radio volume. Dante stood, unsure if he should make a move or just take the hint and leave, Ben obviously wasn't interested.

"Are you just going to stand there watching, or will you help me clean up?" Ben finally yelled above the music, reluctantly turning the volume back to a reasonable decibel.

Dante shook off his suit jacket, laying it over a chair behind the door, and rolled up his shirt sleeves. Ben tossed him a cloth and pointed to the stovetop. It didn't take long to find the cleaning products, and the pair worked away in silence except for the low hum of the radio.

The surfaces gleamed to an almost mirror finish. The last pot and pan had been tucked away. There was nothing else to distract them from the elephant in the room that had grown so big it was almost suffocating.

"So, Ben, I...."

"You don't need to say anything. I can take a hint," Ben quipped.

"And what hint do you think I am giving?"

"You are not interested. I should have realised how long it took you to accept my first invitation."

"No, it's not that...." Dante tried to argue, but Ben interrupted.

"I know I can be a little intense, but I like you. If you were not interested, I would have appreciated being told rather than being offered a pity date."

Dante was stunned. Was that really what he thought? That Dante had only agreed out of pity? It was then that Dante knew how deeply he had hurt Ben.

"It was never a pity date. I'm just.... I.... sometimes struggle with dating, especially when I am forced to admit my feelings...."

"What feelings? You stood me up; clearly, you don't feel the same way I do, and that's fine. I'm happy to keep things strictly professional," Ben said, tossing a hand towel in the hamper.

"You are going to make me beg, aren't you?" Dante joked, seeing the glint in Ben's eyes.

"Only if you want to," Ben winked.

"I will admit, at first, I drastically misjudged you. I thought you were arrogant, lazy, your timekeeping was astonishing...."

"Wow, and here I was thinking this was an apology," Ben laughed, folding his arms across his chest.

"I was wrong. I saw that the first time you came to my defence with Claudia and that horrid friend of hers. Then with all your little gestures, I'm stubborn and don't like admitting when I'm wrong, and as I found the more I saw you, I was starting to warm to you. I got scared. Then our first date was.... beautiful, truly the best first date I have ever been on. You opened up and were so vulnerable, and how did I treat that trust? I freaked out and ran." Dane stopped to take a breath.

"Go on," Ben grinned.

"I realised that I really like you, and I have only ever felt such a rush of feelings once before....it didn't end well, and I was...."

"Scared of getting hurt or being the one to do the hurting," Ben shrugged.

"Exactly. I acted like a child and literally ran out of town to my mother."

Ben erupted into laughter, finally stopping when he saw the uncomfortable look on Dante's face.

"I'm sorry, you were saying?"

"I would like to ask you out on a date. If you can trust that I will turn up this time," Dante finally asked.

"Look, I admire your honesty, and thank you for admitting your flaws. But I'm not interested in wasting my time if you are not really into it."

"I am, I really am. Please. I'll even cook... I'm not as good of a cook as you, but I will try," Dante smiled, his eyes pleading for a second chance.

Ben stood contemplating the decision, making Dante wait in agony before he relaxed and smiled back. Then, the beautiful bright smile lit up his face and eyes. That smile made Dante's stomach flip, skin prickle, and pulse race. Of course he wanted to give Dante a second chance. He wanted it more than anything.

"Si, Guapo. I will go on a date with you."

Ten

DANTE HURRIED AROUND FLUFFING CUSHIONS, straightening picture frames, and checking that every wrinkle and crease had been ironed out of the tablecloth he draped over his small kitchen table. He hadn't invited anyone around to his house in the longest time. His home was his sanctuary, his hideaway from the world, and he expressed himself freely in a way that he felt he couldn't anywhere else. To him, inviting someone into his safe haven was as vulnerable as it got.

The large golden sun-shaped clock on the wall seemed to tick louder than usual. It was like it was mocking Dante, screaming at him that Ben would be around any minute, and that it was far too late to cancel. Checking the pristine kitchen, with all his ingredients laid out, his knives in a perfect line, he started to doubt himself. He was about to cook for one of the most talented chefs in Summershore.

What am I doing? I should have cooked prior to him getting here. What if he thinks my chopping technique is laughable? Why didn't I just order out and plate it up, pretending it was mine? Dante fanned himself with a hand towel, suddenly aware of the heat in his home. He hurried to open the small kitchen windows when he saw Ben's Black Mercedes pull up outside.

Running to the long mirror in the hallway, Dante quickly checked his clothes and hair, freezing momentarily when he heard the doorbell ring. He knew he definitely couldn't avoid Ben now because the small window in the door allowed a brief view inside.

"Hi," Dante smiled, stepping aside to allow Ben to come inside.

Ben smiled widely, holding up a bottle of red wine in one hand and a bottle of white in the other.

"I didn't know what you were cooking, so I brought a few options," Ben smiled.

"That's so lovely, thank you, head through that way; the kitchen is just on the right through the living room," Dante said, closing the door.

Dante needed a second to gather himself. Ben looked amazing. He had made an extra effort to look his best, wearing dark chinos, tan loafers, and a pale grey shirt open at the collar. As he walked past Dante, he could smell his cologne, an intoxicating mix of sandalwood, jasmine, and another scent Dante couldn't quite pinpoint.

"Wow, your home is beautiful. I love the colour scheme," Ben admired.

Dante's home was a mix of turquoise, gold, pale blue, and soft greys. A blend of modern decor with subtle hints of antiques. It had taken Dante years to get everything just how he wanted it, but the wait had been worth it. Every morning when he woke, it was like seeing the finished product for the first time. He loved his home and took so much pride in it.

"Thank you. It's my pride and joy. I feel I can truly express myself here."

Ben followed Dante into the kitchen, perching on one of the white leather bar stools at the central kitchen island.

"So, what is on the menu for tonight?" Ben asked, scanning his eyes over the ingredients laid out before him.

"For starters, I have gazpacho, the main course I'm making duck with a pomegranate glaze, and for dessert, espresso and dark chocolate truffles," Dante answered as he slid the duck into the oven – he had the sense to do most of the prep work before Ben arrived.

"And you say you are not a chef," Ben teased. "You didn't have to go to all this trouble for me. I would have been happy with mac n cheese."

Dante practically slammed the oven door shut, turning to Ben, who was holding in a laugh and failing miserably.

"*Who* told you about that?" Dante gasped with hands on his hips.

"Avery, last time I was at Love and Joy," Ben howled.

Dante was famed for making a mess of his mac n cheese dish for a party he hosted once. Not only had he undercooked the pasta, but he hadn't used the correct measurements of anything, making the dish look like cement. Then, to top it off, he had forgotten he was cooking and burnt the whole thing.

"I'm going to kill her," Dante shook his head, pulling out two wine glasses and a corkscrew.

Dante insisted that Ben not help with the cooking. But after several times when Dante almost chopped off a finger or almost burnt himself on the stove, Ben insisted, if for nothing other than Dante's health and safety. Enjoying good food and great wine, conversation flowed smoothly with any bad blood between them well and truly washed away. Ben told Dane more about his family and his business, explaining how he wasn't really the partying type of guy but had to, occasionally, for his clients or for networking. Dante informed Ben about how he started with Love and joy and the company's plans for the future, with Juliette asking him to look into the process and legalities of franchising. So far, it was all hush-hush, Juliette and Dante agreed to let Avery be the first to be offered her own franchise, but they wanted to make sure it was truly a possibility first. Dante briefly touched on his family history but quickly opted for a subject change. Ben, on the other hand, could not be swayed.

"Hold on, I want to hear more about your family," Ben chuckled.

Dante didn't really want to talk about his family because, especially after one too many glasses of wine, he would get too chatty and most likely reveal a little too much about himself and his fear of marriage.

"There is not much to tell. I don't really talk to my dad, I occasionally get a birthday or Christmas card, and I'm not overly close with my mother. Husband number four saw to that."

"Wow, four times. Have you helped plan any of them?" Ben asked, pouring them both another glass.

"God no! I refuse to have anything to do with her weddings. They are a waste of time; she never sticks with the marriage. She just loves the day's fuss, but the novelty wears off, and soon she's onto the next husband. Weddings are beautiful, and I can't tolerate how she treats them." Dante gulped, suddenly seeing the surprise on Ben's face.

"Sorry," Dante apologized.

"Don't be. You have a passion for what you do. It's one of the biggest things we have in common, and I like that," Ben smiled.

Dante returned Ben's smile but continued to say nothing, wanting to leave the subject where it was.

"Is that truly how you feel? That she just loves the idea of a wedding more than marriage?" Ben finally asked.

Dante thought it over for a moment swirling his wine in his glass. If he was honest with himself, he hadn't given it much thought. He had made his judgement based on what he had seen and how he felt about his job. He had never even asked his mother why none of her marriages worked or why she insisted so hard on finding 'the one'.

"I don't know. I have just spent so much time watching my mother and her string of husbands lose themselves trying to make a marriage work that was never going to. Rather than sitting and assessing the problem, she just jumped onto the next one," Dante admitted.

"Have you ever spoken to her about it?"

"No, it's her business, not mine. But watching her go from husband to husband and both sides experiencing the pain and upheaval in their lives just makes me think marriage isn't for me. It seems like far too much work."

Ben stared back, frozen like a statue with a look of bewilderment on his face that startled Dante, making him shift uncomfortably in his seat.

"I'm sorry if this seems a little out of line, but how can you feel like that when you plan weddings for a living?" Ben asked.

"I love the idea of love, and I love the happiness a wedding brings. It brings out the best in people, and there is so much love, joy, and positivity in that day that makes everything else horrible in the world vanish, even if just for a day. So, I love being a part of that. It's not that I don't believe in marriage; I just don't think it is for me."

"Why?" Ben asked.

Dante felt the same feeling of dread stir in him that had his stomach twisting the day of their original second date. This conversation always made him uncomfortable, and he hated admitting his shortcomings to people or feeling like he had to justify himself. He had spent so much of his life hiding who he was and what he loved to make others happy. When he had finally found himself, it had been a freedom he never wanted to lose.

"It's hard to explain...I think, maybe I just don't want that pain when it fails or to lose myself in a relationship."

"So, if you found your person. The one. Would you never change your mind?"

"Honestly? I've never thought about it. I got close once, but it didn't work, so I went back to my old ways. So, you could say I'm stuck in my ways. A product of ageing, I guess." He smiled.

"Do you want to know what I think?"

"Yes."

"A wedding is just the beginning. It is a statement to the world that this person brings out the best in you, and you do the same to them. It's an equal partnership. If you are forced to be someone you are not in a relationship, then it's never going to work. But when you find that one person, a *marriage* is the most beautiful thing in the world. It's a commitment to someone else's happiness and theirs to yours. You want to help each other thrive and find the beauty in a world that can be so dark. It's an adventure."

Ben's statement stuck in Dante's mind for the rest of the evening. It was plain to see that Ben wanted to get married one day. And for the first time in a long time, Dante began to question what it was about marriage he was so scared of. Ben was a much more profound thinker than Dante had expected, and it amazed him because it made him question his own thinking. Maybe marriage wasn't such a bad thing; after all, the way Ben painted the image was so beautiful that Dante began to think that he could one day change his mind. But as always, doubt crept in.

Was it his feelings or his growing infatuation with Ben?

Eleven

"How did the big date night go?" Juliette asked eagerly.

Dante shrugged but smiled to himself. He hadn't been able to stop thinking about Ben since.

"Not well?" Avery asked, giving Dante a sympathetic look.

Dante shook his head but kept quiet.

"Everything okay?" Juliette asked, turning away from her computer.

"Yeah, it's fine," Dante shrugged, making himself a coffee.

Out of the corner of his eye, he saw Juliette and Avery exchange a worried look. Deciding he didn't want to ask any more questions, he excused himself and headed to his office, closing the door behind him and cracking on with work. No matter how much he tried to keep himself busy, Dante couldn't seem to concentrate. He was starting to really like Ben but didn't want to lead him on. He knew Ben wanted marriage, and Dante still hadn't made up his mind.

He couldn't live with himself if he led the poor guy on but also didn't want to let him go. Slouching in his chair, he ran his hands over his face, conflicted with his feelings. A short soft knock on the door caused him to straighten, waiting for Juliette to walk in.

"You free tonight?" she asked.

"Depends," Dante smiled weakly.

"Mojitos and makeovers? My place? Damian is taking Milo to see a movie, so we have the house to ourselves."

"I don't know," Dante sighed.

"I don't know is not a no," she smiled back.

"You are coming and that final! You are coming if I have to drag you there by that poor excuse for hair you call a beard!" Avery jokingly yelled from the other room.

"Hey! Cheap shot," Dante yelled back, stringing the small goatee, and checking his reflection in his desk's small mirror frame.

"I'll leave you be. We will talk later," Juliette winked, leaving Dante to finally crack on with his to-do list.

Dante finally emerged from his office to find Avery and Juliette waiting with bags full of snacks, drinks, and goodies for the night's festivities. Dante smiled suddenly, feeling so lucky to have such good friends in his life.

"Come on, grumpy pants, get in the car," Avery joked, wrapping an arm around Dante's shoulder.

"Thanks, guys. I think I need a night to let my hair down," Dante grinned.

"Well, don't get too comfortable. I have everything I need in this bag for one of your famous facial scrubs," Juliette raised her bag to highlight her point.

Damian and Milo were already gone by the time everyone got to Juliette's house. A stack of take-out menus lay on the table with three one-hundred-dollar bills. Next to it was a post-it note with the words:

Dinner is on me. Have a great night. D & M xxx

Juliette flicked on the stereo, pumping out classic nineties pop while everyone headed to the bedrooms to get changed into more comfortable clothes. When Dante came downstairs, Juliette was already one step ahead with a pitcher of mojitos waiting and three garnished glasses topped with fun bendy straws in a rainbow of colours and cocktail umbrellas.

"Cheers! To a well-deserved and much overdue get-together," Juliette cheered, raising her glass.

Clicking their glasses, they all took a sip and burst into coughing fits.

"Oh my god, Juliette, are you trying to kill us?" coughed Avery.

"What's wrong?" Juliette stifled a cough, trying to hide her obvious mistake.

"Give it here, my day's woman, you are not supposed to use the entire bottle of gin," teased Dante.

Dante poured out the drinks and started again.

"Here, try this," he said, passing each their new drinks.

"Delicious. A trick you learned from Ben?" Juliette asked, making her eyebrows dance.

"Actually, yes," Dante said, slinking around her and heading to the living room.

That was the gateway to conversation; Dante was all talk once the gin hit him. He felt like a teenager again, gossiping about his latest crush with his besties. Juliette and Avery hung on his every word, listening to Dante tell them how Ben had him feeling and the wonderful conversations they had on their date. Avery and Juliette oohed and awwed when Dante blushed while telling them how Ben had held his hand and showed him the correct way to chop and how he rescued him from almost burning himself. Juliette laughed when Avery defended herself when Dante confronted her about telling Ben the mac and cheese story.

As the night drew on, nails were pained, facial scrubs were done, and hair masks set. They sat cosied up on the sofa in their comfy pj's with their moisturizing sheet masks soaking into their skin on their third pitcher of mojitos when Dante finally felt it was time to confess.

"So, will you tell us why you were bugging out today?" Juliette asked.

Dante took his time before saying it. "He asked my views on marriage, and I said it wasn't for me and how I don't ever want to get married."

Avery and Juliette sat, mouths open and eyes wide, lost for words.

"What? But you love, love. You plan weddings for a living, and you are so good at it," Avery gasped.

"A wedding is just one day, it's everything that comes after that has me concerned. The thing that has me really shaken though, is that.... Ben....in the short time I've actually got to know the real him.... has me questioning everything I ever thought I knew.... It's scary." Dante admitted while fidgeting with the umbrella in his drink.

"You like him a lot, don't you?" Juliette asked.

Dante nodded, his eyes not leaving the swirling ice and mint leaves in his glass.

"That's what worries me. I've watched my mother have whirlwind romances that ended in divorce. I don't want that for me."

"Who says it will?" Avery asked.

Their conversation was interrupted by the pizza delivery guy knocking at the door. Dante was glad for the distraction but felt better for finally opening up to his friends; it felt freeing to no longer carry such a burden alone.

It turned out to be the perfect besties' night. Precisely what all of them needed. As Juliette and Avery danced around the living room, Dante watched with a smile on his face and love in his heart. These girls were all the family he needed. He made a note to make mojito night a regular thing. They didn't do it often enough. Who knew how therapeutic it was to sit around eating food and drinking cocktails with a bit of gossip? They talked, they laughed, and they cried together. It was something they didn't do often enough, only as often as work and life would allow. It had become even harder to get together just the three of them since Juliette and Avery had gotten married, but Dante was grateful for that evening.

Twelve

Mojito night had been exactly what Dante needed, and the following day when he woke, he called Ben and arranged to meet for lunch. He wanted to be honest with him and not make the same mistake again by letting his feelings get in his way.

"*Guapo, Como Estas?*" Ben cheered, kissing Ben softly on the lips as he arrived at *The Golden Coffee Bean*.

"I'm wonderful. I had mojito night with the girls last night, and it was just what I needed. How long do you have? I would like to talk to you about something."

"Oh no! that sounds bad," Ben worried.

"It's not, I promise."

Dante confessed his concerns to Ben. He didn't want to waste Ben's time if Ben was looking for marriage, and while he was working on his issues, he still had a long way to go. Ben sat listening intently, hanging off Dante's every word, soaking it all in.

"I appreciate your honesty. Yes, I would like to get married one day, but who knows what the future holds? So why restrict ourselves to worrying about what may or may not happen? When you concentrate too much on the fear of how something could go wrong, you miss out on the beauty around you," Ben said, reaching for Dante's hand.

"I know, and I'm working on it...."

"No. Please stop worrying, and let's enjoy discovering each other and what this is."

Taking Ben's words to heart, Dante relaxed and stopped asking himself *what if.* Juliette and Avery commented that they had noticed a substantial positive difference in Dante since he had agreed to just take each day at a time. In addition, Claudia's wedding had gone off without a hitch. She had stuck to her word and left a glowing review on her social media about Love and Joy and Ben's catering services for all her followers to see.

Taking away the pressure of worrying about his discomfort around marriage meant that Dante and Ben were free to let their relationship grow at a pace that made them both happy. It wasn't long before their whirlwind romance led them to stay over at each other's houses so much that Ben eventually decided it was better for him to move into Dante's.

Everything felt so natural and not as scary as Dante had feared. Ben became Dante's muse, and it was reflected in all the little subtle details he added to each event. Ben quit his late-night partying with clients and opted for more intimate cocktail hours, most of which Avery organised. Both Love and Joy and Ben's catering services were thriving. Dante lived for how Ben had him thinking deeper about the world. The poetry night at *The Golden Coffee Bean* became a monthly date night that both looked forward to. And the night that Dante finally got up to speak was the night that Juliette, Damian, Avery, and Sarah had joined them.

That same night, Ben proposed. Dante expected to freak out, panic, and run for the hills. But it was the easiest 'yes' he had ever said.

Thirteen

AVERY KEPT her promise and handled everything for Dante's wedding. After the fantastic job he did with her and Sarah's wedding, she wanted to return the favour. Dante wasn't just her manager; he was one of her closest friends. And she knew how much he loved weddings and wanted to give him one he would never forget.

The night before the wedding, Juliette offered for Dante to stay at her house. Avery and Juliette knew that Dante loved Ben, and they could see how happy they made each other. But after Mojitos and makeovers, they also knew that Dante still had some fears around marriage.

"Hey sweetie, we are heading to bed. Do you need anything?" Juliette asked, popping her head into the spare bedroom.

Dante shook his head in response, looking out the window and twisting his bowtie between his fingers.

"Dante? What's up?" Avery asked.

"Nothing, I'm fine," he replied.

Juliette and Avery came to sit on the bed with him, saying nothing, just being there for support. They knew better than to push Dante; he would clam up, so they sat silently, waiting for him to talk.

"I think I've made a mistake. This is all happening too fast. I'm not ready," Dante sighed.

"What's running through your mind?" Avery asked.

"What if Ben isn't the one? What if the novelty of a new relationship wears off and we find we can't stand each other? What if, a few years down the line, Ben realises he has married an old man and wants someone younger? What if...."

"Calm down, sweetie," Juliette said soothingly, stroking Dante's shoulder.

"What if I end up like my mother? Hooked on the wedding feeling and getting divorced after divorce?"

"The fact that you have worried about that for so long should tell you it's not going to happen. You wouldn't let it happen; that's why you have never married before. But look at you and Ben; you fell so deeply in love that you changed your mind on your terms." Avery reassured him.

"If you truly don't want to do this, we will support you. But don't make up your mind when you're feeling so emotional. Think clearly and then make up your mind," Juliette said.

"I think I need to make one of your famous Pro and Cons lists," Dante grinned weakly.

Juliette headed to the draw-in dresser and pulled out a pad and pen. It wasn't long before Dante saw his pros list was overwhelming, and the only thing on his cons list was his fear.

"Thanks, girls, this helped," Dante grinned.

"You know where we are if you need us," Avery smiled.

Sharing a quick group hug, the girls headed off to bed, leaving Dante to read over his list repeatedly. The words seemed to become sharp and threatening; the room felt like the walls were closing in. Suddenly, Dante felt he couldn't breathe; dashing to the window, he flung it open and took several deep breaths, but it didn't help.

"If I have to make a list, I definitely can't do this," he said to the piece of paper before tossing it on the bed.

Grabbing a small bag of his things, he snuck out of Juliette's house and ran.

Fourteen

DANTE SAT IN THE DARK, hiding from the world. His phone hadn't stopped ringing since the sun came up, but each call went ignored. Finally, after a night of little to no sleep and much debating, he managed to shower, eat, and put on his tuxedo. He had hoped it would spark feelings of excitement. But looking at himself in the mirror, all he saw was a failure.

"Ben will hate me," Dante whispered to the empty room, resting his head in his hands.

"No, I won't, Guapo," replied Ben's smooth voice.

Dante's head shot up so fast he heard his neck click; looking over to the door, Ben was leaning against the door frame. His face hidden in the dark. Dante flicked on his desk lamp, finally inviting some light into the room.

"How did you find me?" Dante asked.

"When Juliette said she couldn't find you this morning and you didn't come home last night, I figured work would be the next best place to look. You love this place, and it always helps you think. What's going on, Guapo? Talk to me."

Dante's eyes brimmed with tears as he watched Ben walk across the room dressed in his crisp white suit to sit opposite him. Talking to Ben was never the issue. It was admitting his own downfalls. Ben didn't push; he didn't look angry or hurt. Instead, his eyes held nothing but love. Dante reiterated his concerns from the night before, repeating them, making his anxiety peak. To try and calm his nerves, he paced back and forth behind his desk.

"It's not that I don't want to marry you. I do...."

"Save that line for later," Ben winked with a cheeky grin.

Dante smiled back at him, finally sitting back down.

"It just this fear of us failing is crippling, and I'm going to walk down that beautiful aisle with all those faces on me, who will all be wondering the same thing. Are they rushing in? Are they going to fail? And the thought makes my throat close up," Dante panted feeling lost for breath.

Ben jumped from his seat and grabbed Dante by the shoulders, his only interest was making sure Dante didn't pass out. When Dante was finally calm, Ben knelt before him, resting his hands on his knees.

"If you think this is too fast, we can cancel. If you have any doubt, we can cancel. Just know I don't need a big wedding to tell the world I'm spending the rest of my life with you. If marriage feels like a cage, we won't do it. I just want to be with you."

"You would do that for me?" Dante gasped.

"Of course. Yes, I love the idea of marriage, but I love the idea of us more. I just wanted you to have a day as special as the days you give to others."

Dante was overwhelmed with gratitude for the sacrifice Ben was willing to make. He was ready to give up his dream to make him happy; it warmed his heart and then sent a jolt of fear and dread through him.

"No, that's exactly it. I don't want you to give up your dream to please me. That's what I feared marriage would do, change us," Dante panicked.

"You are my dream. Not a piece of paper and a ring. I'm in no matter what you decide. You are not getting rid of me that easy. This is your choice."

"You truly love me, don't you?" Dante asked as if it was the first time hearing the words.

"More than anything."

"I want to be with you, and I want to give you your dream, but....Oh no, it's bad luck for us to see each other before the wedding!"

"Is it the big wedding? All that pressure? Because to me, it sounds like you want this marriage."

Dante thought it over; perhaps his fear was routed in the judgement of others, the pressure of building a successful marriage around one big perfect day. A day he tried to get perfect for everyone because his parents' marriage fell apart, even though their wedding day was beautiful. *That's it.* He thought. *I have been wrong this whole time!*

"I think you are right," Dante breathed. *A day can't make or break something so special.*

"Leave it with me," Ben winked.

Ben left Dante's office at Love and Joy, leaving Dante to think over everything Ben had said. With the kind words, and the heart-felt gesture, he considered himself so lucky to have found someone to make him so happy, and he wanted to do the same for Ben.

Running out of his office and into the main storefront, Dante froze. Juliette, Damian, Avery, Sarah, Emma, and Milo were all dressed and waiting. A makeshift altar had been erected in the foyer, and Ben stood talking with an efficient.

"What is all this?" Dante gasped.

"It was supposed to be a surprise," Milo chimed.

"We do not need a huge fancy wedding ceremony. All we need is the love of our closest friends and family and each other. Then, everyone else can wait until the reception to celebrate with us." Ben smiled.

"This is perfect. I can't believe you managed to pull it all off so quickly."

"I said one day I would have the honour of planning your wedding; I always had backup plans," Avery winked.

"Thank you," Dante mouthed.

"So Dante, I ask you again. Will you marry me?" Ben took Dante's hands in his.

"I do," Dante beamed, "Oh wait, I should be saving that line for later," he winked back.

The ceremony was perfect. The world melted away, leaving only Dante and Ben with those they truly loved to share in their perfect magical moment. However, Dante had a surprise for Ben. When it came to the vows, he had written them in Spanish; it was a small gesture, but a gesture that had Ben overwhelmed. As Dante spoke his words, Ben translated for their guests. There wasn't a dry eye in the room.

"It gives me great pleasure. To present Mr. & Mr. Smith-Ramos," said the beaming officiant.

The room erupted in cheers, claps, and confetti poppers being pulled. It wasn't the wedding he had ever imagined for himself, but it was more than he could have ever asked for. It was perfect. Love and Joy had changed his life; it was only fitting that he celebrated the next significant chapter there.

His dream job, his new family, and the love swelled in the room. Love and Joy had brought everything to all of their lives. Damian and Juliette were trying for a baby, and Sarah and Avery had finally received the good news about adopting their son. Dante looked forward to what milestone he and Ben would celebrate next.

"Juliette, you couldn't have named this place anything better. Our lives are bursting with Love and Joy," Dante hugged her.

"I'm just glad I got to see your love and joy for myself. You deserve it so much," she hugged back.

The End.
Did you enjoy *Something Blue*?
Please consider rating it on Bookbub, Goodreads or your favorite retailer.
Reviews help me reach new readers.

Join my Newsletter on www.daisylandishromance.com for updates and giveaways!

Sneak Peak

Grounded for Christmas

A freaking *storm*.

This was just what Jamie needed. She might have manifested it by thinking there was no way this day could get worse a few times since that morning; she had stepped in dog poo, cracked her phone screen, and got into an argument with her manager.

And now, it looked like she'd be stranded at JFK for an undetermined amount of time. The *DELAYED* displayed in red letters on the boarding gate screen mocked her. Her shoulders slumped with the heavy sigh flitting past her lips as she scanned the crowded waiting area, then the next one over. It seemed like her plane was not the only one stuck to the ground. She didn't spot any vacant seats.

She opted to sit on the floor in a relatively quiet corner next to a power socket as she knew her phone was about to die. *If I'm going to wait for several hours, I will definitely need some entertainment.* The only downside of the elected spot was that Jamie soon realized it was located right underneath a speaker playing Christmas music. The thought of enduring merry tunes for the next few hours or so positively made her skin crawl, but every other plug was taken. Jamie accepted her fate.

You guessed it: Jamie was *not* a Christmas person. Having her parents go through an ugly divorce during the holiday when she was ten might have had something to do with it. Followed closely by having to choose where to spend it: in rainy, depressing Seattle with her alcoholic mom, or in humid, homophobic Arlington with her dad, the step-monster, and the evil step-twins.

So yeah, it was safe to say that this particular holiday was not Jamie's favorite time of the year. She couldn't have cared less about being stuck at the airport on Christmas Eve; any other day would have been just as annoying, though less crowded.

She briefly registered someone sitting a few feet to her right as she tugged her scarf off her neck, then grabbed her large handbag to fish for her charger.

"Shoot," she muttered when, after emptying its contents on the floor, the item was nowhere to be found. She must have left it plugged in at the hotel. "This is perfect. Absolutely perfect."

She checked her phone next and groaned, the five percent battery level glaring at her reproachfully.

"Everything okay?"

The soft voice drew her attention to her right. Her jaw damn near fell out of its hinges when she met the most vibrant blue eyes she'd ever seen. Her brain stalled and she realized she must have looked like a fish out of water with her mouth trying to form words but no sound coming out.

"Sorry," she eventually managed, releasing a strained chuckle. *If the stranger is creeped out, she doesn't let it show.* "I uh, I forgot my charger at the hotel, and my phone is dying."

Now there's a first-world problem, she realized as the words came out of her mouth.

"Oh. What kind of phone do you have?"

"Um, the iPhone 5," she sayd, holding it up. "I know, I'm a dinosaur."

The redhead laughed and unplugged her phone, handing her charger to Jamie a few seconds later. "Here."

Jamie hesitantly took it, eyeing the other woman. "You sure you don't need it?"

"I'm at fifty-six percent, so I'll be fine for a bit. We can just switch on and off; it seems like we're going to be here for a while."

Jamie released another groan as she tilted her head back against the wall. "Ugh. This day couldn't get any worse."

Shoot. She better keep her mouth shut, or a meteor might hit them next.

"Tell me about it," the stranger muttered, letting out a dry chuckle.

"Thanks," Jamie said, lifting the charger still held in her hand. "I appreciate it."

"No sweat," the other woman assured her, then paused. "I'm Emma, by the way."

Jamie nodded, smiling a little. "Jamie. Great to meet you."

"You too. Going or leaving home?"

"Heading home. I live in L.A.," Jamie replied as she plugged in her phone, resting it on her lap for now as there was no point using it when the battery is still so low. "You?"

"Same."

Jamie nodded once more. She didn't know what pushed her to encourage conversation. She was pretty much allergic to people and tended to keep to herself, but there was something about Emma that just... drew her in. And no, it's not because she was likely the most beautiful person Jamie had ever seen. There was more to it than Jamie had yet to pinpoint. "So, what was so bad about your day?" She asked after a beat.

"I flew out here to get my stuff from my ex's apartment."

Jamie's nose crinkled in a grimace. She instantly regretted asking that question. "Ouch, sorry."

Emma waved off her concern with her hand. "It's fine. We broke up a while ago while I was doing my internship in L.A.," she explained. "I got an excellent job offer, and long-distance was already tricky. We decided it was best to end things before it got too ugly."

Jamie nodded slowly. "Gotcha. What do you do?"

"I'm a vet. You?"

"Oh, uh, I make music." That sounded way like someone making covers on YouTube. She tried again, "I'm a music producer."

Emma's eyes lit up at that. "Really? What kind?"

"Mostly pop."

She tilted her head to the side. "Anything I might have heard?"

"Um, do you know Addison Rain?"

"Have I been living under a rock?" Emma challenged with a smirk. "Of course I do! You're her producer?"

Jamie nodded, her cheeks heating a little. "On her last track, yeah."

"That's very cool." Jamie only shrugged. It's always awkward receiving compliments. "You like to listen to her music, then?"

Jamie's brow furrowed over the odd question. "Um yeah? That's... kind of a given since I produced the thing."

"Oh, you don't know."

"Huh?" Her frown only deepened in confusion. "Know what?"

Emma grinned, trapping her bottom lip between her teeth for a beat. "If someone wants to know whether a girl is into girls, that someone should ask her if she listens to Addison Rain. It's like... a thing."

Jamie's brain took its sweet time registering the meaning behind Emma's words. The lightbulb eventually flicked on, and her jaw slowly dropped, a flush rushing to meet her face and down her neck.

"Oh," was all she could manage, pinching her lips together as she broke eye contact before she died from overheating.

GAWD, I'm such a gay disaster. Someone should take away my license.

Continue Reading
Grounded for Christmas
https://mybook.to/groundedforchristmas